From Poverty to Prosperity

Poems of Hope and Resilience

From Poverty to Prosperity: Poems of Hope and Resilience

by

Marlon McIntyre

Published in 2023 by Tamarind Hill Press

ISBN:

Paperback - 978-1-915161-41-3

eBook - 978-1-915161-37-6

Tamarind Hill Press Limited

Copies are available at special rates for bulk orders. Contact us on email at info@tamarindhillpress.co.uk or by phone on +44 1325 775 255 OR +44 7982 90 90 37 for more information.

**TAMARiND HiLL
.PRESS**

CONTENTS

Preface..7

Rising Above the Struggles 10

The Power of Education 12

Dreams of a Better Life..14

Overcoming Adversity..16

Hope in the Darkness...18

The Path to Success...20

A New Beginning 23

Breaking Free 26

The Strength Within 28

The Road to Opportunity 30

Pushing Past the Limits..32

Rising from the Ashes 34

Finding Your Purpose 37

The Promise of Tomorrow 40

Building Your Future 43

Learning to Fly..46

Believe in Yourself...49

Unlocking Your Potential 53

Never Giving Up..55

The Journey of Self-Discovery 57

Pursuing Your Passion 59

The Courage to Succeed 61

Overcoming Fear...63

The Beauty of Perseverance 65

Dare to Dream 67

The Art of Resilience 69

Embracing Change 71

The Magic of Imagination 74

The Power of Positivity 77

The Gift of Gratitude 79

The Joy of Giving Back 81

The Importance of Hard Work 83

The Call to Action 85

The Freedom to Choose 87

The Courage to Follow Your Heart 89

From Poverty to Prosperity 91

Preface

Growing up in poverty can be a daunting challenge, and it can feel like the deck is stacked against you. However, it is possible to overcome these obstacles and achieve your dreams with hard work, resilience, and determination. The poems in this collection are a testament to that, as they are inspired by my personal journey of rising *From Poverty to Prosperity*.

Through my own story, I share a message of hope and encouragement to young adults who are facing similar struggles. The poems in this book were all written between my teenage years in high school and a few years ago. The last poem in the book was written back in 2022. It was this poem that made me think of digging up all my poems and seeing whether a publisher would be interested in them. I am grateful to have been offered a contract with Tamarind Hill Press, so that I can share these poems with you, and look forward to sharing more.

The poems in this collection offer unique perspectives on how to overcome adversity and unlock one's full potential. They are meant to inspire you to pursue your dreams and never give up, regardless of the challenges you face.

The themes of hope and perseverance that run throughout this book are meant to remind you that you are capable of achieving anything you set your mind to. Whether it is through education, hard work, or simply believing in oneself, success is possible.

After each poem, I have added a quote of inspiration from someone else. I have done this because I want you to realise that

MANY of us have been where you are, so you can get to where we are and even 'outrun' us.

As you read through these poems, may they serve as a source of inspiration and motivation on your own journey towards prosperity. May they remind you that you have the strength and power within you to overcome any obstacle and create the life you want.

Enjoy the poems, and if you like them, don't forget to leave a review online. Thank you, and I wish you nothing but the best. You've got this. You are capable of doing anything and becoming anything.

"If I give up now, I will spend the rest of my life wondering 'what if' and that will be an even bigger waste of my time."

\-   Marlon McIntyre

Rising Above the Struggles

When life knocks you down, don't give up the fight

For there's a strength within you, burning bright

It may be hard to see, in the midst of strife

But it's the spark that ignites, the fire of life.

Rising above the struggles, takes courage and grit

But the journey is worth it, don't you dare quit

For the view from the top, is breath-taking and grand

And you'll be proud of the person, you've come to understand.

Don't let your circumstances, define who you are

You're stronger than you think, reach for the stars

Believe in yourself, and what you can achieve

And watch as your dreams, start to manifest and breathe.

"You may encounter many defeats but do not be defeated. In fact, it may be necessary to encounter the defeats, so you can know who you are, what you can rise from, how you can still come out of it."

-    Maya Angelou

The Power of Education

Education is the key to unlock the door

To a world of possibilities never seen before.

It's the fuel that drives your passions and dreams

And helps you reach the highest of extremes

The power of education is not just in the books

It's in the lessons learned and the skills it took

To navigate the world with confidence and grace

And embrace the challenges that you'll soon face

Open your mind and let the learning begin

For the power of education is a life-changing win

It can take you places you never thought you'd go

And help you become the best version of you, you know

"Education is the most powerful weapon which you can use to change the world."

- Nelson Mandela

Dreams of a Better Life

I dream of a better life—one without pain or strife,

A world of endless possibilities where I can thrive,

Where the sky is the limit and the stars shine bright

And I can make my dreams a reality in sight.

I won't let my circumstances hold me back or down,

For I have the power to turn things around.

With hard work and determination, I'll pave the way

To a life full of promise each and every day.

My dreams are my fuel, my motivation and drive,

They keep me going, and help me survive.

Through the highs and lows, the ups and downs,

I'll keep chasing my dreams till I wear the crown.

Bring on the challenges, the obstacles and fear

I won't let them stop me; I'll persevere.

For I believe in myself and what I can achieve,

And my life can become anything my mind can conceive.

"So many of our dreams at first seem impossible, then seem improbable, and then, when we summon the will, they soon seem inevitable."

\-   Christopher Reeve

Overcoming Adversity

I've faced my share of adversity in this journey of life

But I won't let it define me or hold me back from the light

For I have the strength within me to rise above it all

And turn my struggles into victories, no matter how small.

The road has been bumpy with twists and turns galore

But each challenge I've overcome has only made me more

Determined to succeed and live life to the fullest extent

And show the world that my life is my own event.

Overcoming adversity takes courage and grit

But it's the lessons learned that help us fit

Into the person we're destined to be

Strong, resilient, and truly free.

Now, I'll keep on pushing and never give up the fight

For I know that, in the end, everything will be alright

And I'll look back on my journey with pride and love,

Knowing that I've overcome adversity, with the strength from above.

"We must not wish for the disappearance of our troubles but for the grace to transform them."

\-   Simone Weil

Hope in the Darkness

When the world seems dark and the road is rough

I hold on to hope that I'll soon find enough

To light up my path and guide me through

The darkness and shadows that obscure my view.

Hope is my beacon, my guiding star

It leads me forward, no matter how far

And though the journey may be long and hard

I know that hope will always stand guard.

Through the trials and tribulations that life may bring

I'll hold on to hope and spread my wings

For hope is the light that illuminates the way

And brings joy and peace at the end of the day.

I'll never give up and never lose sight

Of the hope that burns with a brilliant light

For it's the hope in the darkness that helps us find

Our way to a brighter future and a peaceful mind.

"Sometimes the most healing thing to do is remind ourselves over and over and over, other people feel this too."

\-   Andrea Gibson

The Path to Success

The path to success is not an easy one

It's full of obstacles that must be overcome

But, with hard work and dedication, I know I'll make it through

And achieve my dreams, no matter what I must do.

The journey may be long and the road may be tough

But I won't let that stop me, I'll just strut my stuff

With a determined spirit, and a can-do attitude

I'll find my way and break down each interlude.

Success is not just a destination, it's a state of mind,

It's the culmination of all the hard work we leave behind

And though the journey may be hard, and the climb may be steep,

I'll keep on pushing forward with my eyes on the prize that I'll reap.

Each step I take brings me closer to my goal

And every challenge I face, makes me stronger as a whole,

For success is not just about what we achieve in the end,

It's the journey we undertake and the lessons we comprehend.

I'll keep on striving with all my heart and soul

And never give up until I reach my ultimate goal,

For the path to success is not just a destination to find,

It's the journey we embark on with a steadfast mind.

"The only limit to our realization of tomorrow will be our doubts of today."

- Franklin D. Roosevelt

A New Beginning

A new beginning, a fresh start

A chance to mend a broken heart

To leave the past behind, and start anew

With hope and joy in all that we pursue.

The slate is clean, the future bright

And though the road may seem out of sight

We take that first step, with a heart full of hope

And find the courage to learn and to cope.

A new beginning is not just a dream

It's a choice we make to change the scene

To leave the darkness and embrace the light

And find the strength to take on the fight.

For life is full of twists and turns

And sometimes we stumble, and sometimes we learn

But a new beginning is a chance to grow

To find the path that we want to follow.

Let's seize this moment with all our might

Knowing that happiness, success, and wealth is our birth right,

For a new beginning is a gift we can't ignore

A chance to start anew, and find what we're looking for.

"Change can be scary, but you know what's scarier? Allowing fear to stop you from growing, evolving, and progressing."

-       Mandy Hale

Breaking Free

I'm breaking free from the chains that bind

The fear and doubt that cloud my mind

It's time to let go of all that holds me back

And find the courage to follow the right track.

For too long, I've been living in fear

Afraid to chase my dreams and persevere

But now I realize that it's time to take a chance

And break free from this negative trance.

I'll spread my wings and soar to the sky

With determination and hope, I'll give it a try

And though the journey may be hard and long

I know I can, so I'll stay strong.

So, here's to breaking free from all that holds me down

To chasing my dreams, with a purpose profound

For life is too short to waste on fears and doubt

I'm ready to break free, even if I have to live without.

"Breaking free, or not, is usually determined by whether you want to get somewhere slowly or nowhere fast."

- Tonya Hurley

The Strength Within

The strength within is a force to be reckoned with

A fire that burns bright and never quits,

It's the will to succeed and the courage to try

To stand tall and strong, with my head held high.

Life may be tough, and the road may be long

But I know I'm capable, and I'll stay strong

With the strength within, I can conquer all

And rise above the challenges, big or small.

For the strength within is not just a power,

It's a mindset that fuels and empowers

To believe in myself, and all that I can be

To never give up, and always strive to be free.

I'll continue to harness the strength within, and let it shine

To chase my dreams, and reach for the divine

For with the strength within, I can achieve it all

And rise above, no matter how big or small.

"My dark days made me strong. Or maybe I already was strong, and they made me prove it."

\-   Emery Lord

The Road to Opportunity

The road to opportunity is not an easy one

It's full of twists and turns, and battles to be won

But with a determined spirit, and a will to succeed

We can find our way, and plant the seed.

The journey may be long, and the path may be unclear

But we'll find the way, and overcome the fear

For the road to opportunity is paved with hope

And with every step, we'll learn and grow.

The doors of opportunity are waiting to be opened

And with the right attitude, we'll never be broken

For the road to opportunity is not just a path to follow

It's a chance to create, and pave our own tomorrow.

Let's take that first step and never look back

For the road to opportunity is what we make of the track

With hard work and dedication, we can achieve our dreams

And rise above, no matter how hard it seems.

"Turn your obstacles into opportunities and your problems into possibilities."

- Roy T. Bennett

Pushing Past the Limits

I push past the limits with everything I can muster,

Embracing difficulties but also life's splendour

There's a long road ahead that I have to walk

And I'll keep on going, I will not balk.

I know that the journey won't be an easy one

But I'll keep on pushing till the task is done,

I'll face the challenges that come my way

And I'll overcome them day after day.

I won't allow fear to get in my way

I'll keep on moving come what may,

I'll keep on pushing through life's demands

And I'll make it happen with my own two hands.

I'll rise up high and I'll stand my ground,

I'll keep on pushing till I turn things around,

I'll make a difference with all of my heart,

And I'll keep on going till the day I depart.

"All of my past challenges have helped me become who I am today."

-       Demo Lovato

Rising from the Ashes

Rising from the ashes,

Like a phoenix reborn,

I emerged from the darkness,

My spirit newly formed.

I faced the flames of struggle,

And burned with pain and fear,

But I refused to crumble,

And let my dreams disappear.

With every trial and tribulation,

I grew stronger in my soul,

And found the determination,

To reach my ultimate goal.

My heart was once shattered,

And my hopes were nearly lost,

But I picked up the pieces,

And refused to pay the cost.

I shed the weight of my past,

And embraced a new beginning,

I dared to break the mould,

And let my true self sing.

I rose up from the ashes,

A blazing symbol of hope,

My spirit unbreakable,

My dreams within my scope.

I'll never forget my struggles,

And the journey that brought me here,

For it's through my darkest moments,

That I discovered my truest gear.

So let the fires rage on,

And let the ashes fall,

For I am a phoenix reborn,

And I'll rise above it all.

"I can be changed by what happens to me. But I refuse to be reduced by it."

- Maya Angelou

Finding Your Purpose

I searched for my purpose

In the depths of my heart and soul,

To find my true calling,

And let my spirit take control.

I wandered through the shadows,

And braved the stormy seas,

But I kept my heart open,

And allowed myself to be.

I discovered my passion,

And let it guide my way,

And every step I took,

Led me closer to a brighter day.

I learned to trust my instincts

And let my heart lead the way,

And every time I stumbled,

I rose again with newfound faith.

For when we find our purpose,

Our spirit ignites with a blaze,

And the world becomes a canvas

For us to paint our life's beautiful maze.

"Your vision will become clear only when you can look into your own heart. Who looks outside, dreams; who looks inside, awakes."

-    Carl Jung

The Promise of Tomorrow

The promise of tomorrow,

Is a light that shines so bright,

And it fills my heart with hope,

And sets my soul alight.

I face each new day with courage,

And embrace the unknown with grace,

For I know that every challenge,

Leads me to a brighter space.

I let go of all my fears,

And welcome the winds of change,

For with every shift and turn,

A new opportunity I'll arrange.

The promise of tomorrow,

Is a seed that we must sow,

And with each passing moment,

Our dreams and passions grow.

Now, let us take each step with faith,

And let our hearts be our guide,

For with the promise of tomorrow,

Our spirits will always rise.

"Resist your fear; fear will never lead to you a positive end. Go for your faith and what you believe."

-    T. D. Jakes

Building Your Future

To build a future bright,

You must first lay down your roots,

With every brick and stone,

And every seed you sow and nurture with your boots.

You must cultivate your vision,

And let it guide your way,

And with every passing moment,

Your future takes shape, day by day.

You'll face challenges and setbacks,

And some moments will feel like defeat,

But you must keep your heart open,

Put your determination in the driver's seat.

For when you build your future,

You're crafting a legacy of your own,

And with every step you take,

Your spirit grows and is honed.

Face each day with purpose,

And let your passion be your fuel,

For building your future is a journey,

That takes heart, soul, and will.

"Your future is created by what you do today, not tomorrow."

-       Robert Kiyosaki

Learning to Fly

Learning to fly

Is a journey that takes time,

And it starts with a dream

And a belief that you can climb.

You must spread your wings

And let your spirit take flight,

And with every gust of wind,

You'll grow stronger with all your might.

You'll face moments of doubt

And times when you'll feel afraid,

But you must keep your eyes forward

And let your soul's courage blaze.

For when you learn to fly

Your spirit will soar so high,

And the world becomes a playground

For you to explore, reach, and try.

So let your heart be your compass

And let your dreams be your guide,

For learning to fly is a journey

That fills your spirit with pride.

"There will be obstacles. There will be doubters. There will be mistakes. But with hard work, there are no limits."

- Michael Phelps

Believe in Yourself

Believe in yourself,

And let your heart lead the way,

For when you trust in your abilities,

Your spirit's flame ignites with a beautiful flare.

You must see the potential within,

Allow hope to nurture your abilities,

For when you believe in yourself,

The world becomes a canvas of endless possibilities.

You'll face moments of darkness,

And times when you'll feel lost,

But you must keep your faith strong,

Don't let your future pay the ultimate cost.

For when you believe in yourself,

You unlock a power so strong,

That nothing can hold you back,

And your heart sings its beautiful song.

And never let the doubts of others

Bring down your dreams or your soul,

For you have the power within you

To reach any goal.

Believe in your talents and gifts

And trust in your unique path,

For with hard work and determination,

Success is within your grasp.

Let your faith be your anchor,

And let your courage be your guide,

For when you believe in yourself,

The world is yours to stride.

Remember that challenges and setbacks

Are just stepping stones on your way,

And with every obstacle you overcome,

You grow stronger every day.

Believe in yourself

And trust that you can achieve anything,

For with persistence and positivity,

You'll just be soaring.

"The moment you doubt whether you can fly, you cease forever to be able to do it."

- J.M. Barrie

Unlocking Your Potential

Deep inside of me lies a seed,

A potential waiting to be freed,

A unique talent and ability,

A power that I must see.

I know that there are challenges ahead,

And doubts that fill my head,

But I have the courage to push through,

And unlock my potential, that's true.

I will work hard and persevere,

To conquer every challenge and fear,

And let my talent and ability,

Guide me to my destiny.

For I know that with hard work and focus,

And determination that never loses,

I can achieve my wildest dreams,

And unlock my potential that gleams.

"Your past is not your potential. In any hour you can choose to liberate the future."

\-   Marilyn Ferguson

Never Giving Up

In life, there are times when we fall,

And it seems like we have lost it all,

But it's in those moments that we must rise,

And never give up on our prize.

Though the road may be long and steep,

And the obstacles may make us weep,

We must keep moving forward still,

With the strength of our will.

We may stumble and fall along the way,

But we must rise and fight another day,

For in our heart we hold the key,

To never give up on our destiny.

And when we reach the top of the mountain,

And look back on the journey that we've been on,

We'll know that every step was worth it,

For we never gave up in our spirit.

"Nothing is impossible. The word itself says: 'I'm possible!'"

\-   Audrey Hepburn

The Journey of Self-Discovery

In the depths of my soul, I seek,

A journey that's unique,

A path that's full of wonder and delight,

And a purpose that feels just right.

I'll search high and low, and near and far,

For the answers to the questions in my heart,

And in the process, I'll find,

The beauty that lies within my mind.

I'll embrace the highs and lows,

And the lessons that life bestows,

And in the end, I'll find my way,

To the path that leads to what's meant to be.

And as I journey through life with grace,

And courage in my heart to face

Every challenge that comes my way,

I know that everything will turn out okay.

"Knowing yourself is the beginning of all wisdom."

\-   Aristotle

Pursuing Your Passion

Deep in my heart lies a fire,

A passion that never tires,

A dream that I can't ignore,

And a purpose that I must explore.

I'll chase my passion with all my might,

And work hard day and night,

To make it a reality,

And to find true prosperity.

I'll never let go of my dream,

Or let others' doubts and fears intervene,

For my passion is my guiding star,

And it will take me very far.

And when I finally reach the peak,

Of the mountain that I seek,

I'll know that I did it my way,

And my passion was worth the fray.

"No success was won without enthusiasm and perseverance."

\-   Lailah Gifty Akita

The Courage to Succeed

In the face of fear and doubt,

I'll stand tall and shout

That I have the courage to succeed,

And the strength to conquer every deed.

I'll face every challenge head on

With the courage to keep moving on,

And the faith to believe

That I can achieve anything I conceive.

I'll never let fear hold me back,

Or let doubt cause me to crack,

For my courage is my greatest ally,

And it will take me to the sky.

And when I look back on the road I've travelled,

And the challenges that I have unravelled,

I'll know that my courage and faith,

Were the keys to my success in every race.

"Success means having the courage, the determination, and the will to become the person you believe you were meant to be."

-    George A. Sheehan

Overcoming Fear

I stand before the world, trembling with fright,

My heart races with every step I take,

But I know that I must not give up the fight,

For my dreams are too important to forsake.

I take a deep breath, and I close my eyes,

And I remind myself of all that I can do,

I let go of my doubts and my fears and my lies,

And I focus on the goal that I pursue.

I take another step, and then another one,

And I feel the fear begin to fade away,

For I am stronger than I thought I could become,

And I am capable of seizing the day.

And as I conquer my fears, one by one,

I feel my confidence begin to grow,

For I know that I have what it takes to get things done,

And I am ready to let my greatness show.

"It's OKAY to be scared. Being scared means you're about to do something really, really brave."

- Mandy Hale

The Beauty of Perseverance

Life is a journey filled with ups and downs,

And sometimes the road is long and hard,

But if we keep on pushing, and we don't let go,

We will find the beauty in everything, even let down our guard.

We will find the strength to carry on,

Even when the path seems steep and dark,

For we know that our will is strong,

And our passion will light the spark.

We will learn from every setback,

And we will rise from every fall,

For we know that every challenge we face,

Is an opportunity to give it our all.

And as we keep on moving forward,

Through the sunshine and the rain,

We will discover the beauty of perseverance,

And the power of our inner flame.

"It always seems impossible until it's done."

— Nelson Mandela

Dare to Dream

I close my eyes and I see a world of possibility,

A world where I am free to be whoever I want to be,

Where my dreams are not just fantasies, but a reality,

And I am filled with a sense of wonder and vitality.

I see myself soaring high above the clouds,

Dancing to the rhythm of my heart's desires,

Breaking down the barriers that once held me down,

And lighting up the world with my inner fire.

I know that the road will not be easy,

And there will be times when I will want to quit,

But I will never lose sight of my vision,

For it is what gives me strength and grit.

I dare to dream of a better tomorrow,

Where I am happy, fulfilled, and free,

And I know that as long as I keep on believing,

My dreams will become my reality.

"Never give up on what you really want to do. The person with big dreams is more powerful than one with all the facts."

\-   Albert Einstein

The Art of Resilience

Life is not always kind, and sometimes we fall,

But that's not the measure of our character—no, not at all,

It is in the way we rise up and stand tall,

And how we make the world recognise our footfall.

We learn the art of resilience through our struggles,

Through the pain, the heartbreak, and the strife,

For it is in those moments that we find our muscles,

And we discover the depths of our own inner life.

And as we walk through the valleys and the hills,

And we face the challenges that come our way,

We know that we have the power and the will,

To turn any night into a beautiful day.

"Even if I knew that tomorrow the world would go to pieces, I would still plant my apple tree."

\-   Martin Luther

Embracing Change

I used to fear the unknown,

To cling to what was familiar and safe,

But life is full of surprises,

And change is an inevitable part of the race.

I used to resist the winds of change,

To hold on tight to what I knew,

But I've learned that change can be a gift,

And that growth often comes from something new.

Embracing change can be a challenge,

But it can also be a chance to thrive,

To step outside of our comfort zones,

And to truly come alive.

Sometimes change is forced upon us,

And we must adapt or fall behind,

But even when change is unwelcome,

We can choose the way we respond in kind.

Embracing change can mean letting go,

Of things we thought we could not live without,

But it can also mean gaining so much more,

And finding a new way to move about.

I choose to embrace the winds of change,

To dance in the midst of uncertainty,

To trust that life has a plan for me,

And to move forward with positivity.

"Those who expect moments of change to be comfortable and free of conflict have not learned their history."

- Joan Wallach Scott

The Magic of Imagination

I close my eyes and let my mind roam free,

Into a world that only I can see,

A place where anything is possible,

And the only limit is my own ability.

In this realm of infinite possibility,

My imagination is my greatest tool,

With it, I can create whole new worlds,

And bring to life characters so cool.

I can imagine myself as a hero,

Fighting against impossible odds,

Or I can imagine myself as a wizard,

Casting spells with a flick of my wand.

In my mind's eye, I can explore the depths of space,

Or delve into the mysteries of the deep blue sea,

I can travel through time and witness history,

Or visit lands of myth and fantasy.

My imagination is my secret weapon,

A source of inspiration and delight,

It helps me to dream big and reach for the stars,

And to see the world in a brand new light.

With my imagination, I can make the impossible possible,

And turn the ordinary into something grand,

It helps me to see the world with wonder,

And to understand the power of my own hand.

So, I cherish the gift of imagination,

And I hold it close each and every day,

For with it, I can create a world of magic,

And bring to life the dreams that come my way.

"Everything you can imagine is real."

-    Pablo Picasso

The Power of Positivity

I've learned that positivity is key

To living life in harmony,

For when I focus on the good,

I can overcome anything I should.

Even when the days are tough,

And it seems like things are rough,

I choose to see the brighter side,

And let my inner light guide.

With a positive attitude in tow,

I can turn any obstacle into a foe,

And emerge victorious in the end,

With the strength of my mind to lend.

I'll always choose positivity,

And let it fill me with serenity,

For it's the foundation of my might,

And the key to living life just right.

"Be thankful for what you have; you'll end up having more. If you concentrate on what you don't have, you will never, ever have enough."

- Oprah Winfrey

The Gift of Gratitude

Gratitude is a precious gift,

That I try to practice and uplift,

For it reminds me of all I have,

And the blessings that abound and add.

Even on the hardest of days,

I find something for which to give thanks and praise,

And as I do, my heart expands,

With joy, peace, and love at hand.

For gratitude is more than words,

It's a feeling that uplifts and stirs,

And as I focus on all with what I'm blessed,

I find that I'm more content and less stressed.

I'll keep giving thanks each day,

For all the blessings that come my way,

And let the gift of gratitude

Fill my heart with joy at its greatest magnitude.

"The real gift of gratitude is that the more grateful you are, the more present you become."

- Robert Holden

The Joy of Giving Back

There's joy in giving, I've found,

For it spreads love and kindness all around,

And as I help others in need,

I find that my heart is filled with a different kind of greed.

Not for wealth or material things,

But for the joy that giving brings,

For when I see a smile on another's face,

I know that I'm in the right place.

And as I give with all my heart,

I find that I'm never apart,

From the beauty and grace of life,

And all the good that comes in strife.

I'll keep giving with all I am,

For the joy that it brings and the peace it can,

And let the joy of giving back,

Fill my heart with love and peace that never lack.

"Volunteers don't get paid, not because they're worthless, but because they're priceless."

\-   Sherry Anderson

The Importance of Hard Work

Hard work is the path to success,

The key to achieving all that we profess,

For when we put in the time and effort,

We can accomplish all the goals that we set.

Even when the road is long and hard,

And the journey seems to go on unmarred,

We can always find the strength inside,

To keep pushing forward with nothing to hide.

For hard work is more than just a task,

It's a way of life that we must grasp,

And as we do, we find the key,

To unlocking all that we can be.

So, I'll keep working hard each day,

And let my dedication pave the way,

To a life that's filled with all I need,

And the happiness that comes from doing the deed.

"Hard work beats talent when talent doesn't work hard."

-    Tim Notke

The Call to Action

I hear the call to action,

A voice that echoes in my soul,

It urges me to take a step,

And make my broken pieces whole.

The road ahead may be unclear,

And fear may try to hold me back,

But I know I have the strength,

To rise above and stay on track.

I'll take a deep breath and begin,

With small steps that lead to more,

For every action that I take,

Brings me closer to what I'm fighting for.

And so, I'll heed the call to action,

With courage and conviction in my heart,

I'll chase my dreams and make them real,

And create a life that's full of art.

"If you want something new, you have to stop doing something old."

\-   Peter Drucker

The Freedom to Choose

I have the freedom to choose

The path that I will take,

I have the power to decide

The kind of life I want to make.

No one can dictate to me

The direction in which I go,

For only I can chart my course

And make my own life's flow.

With every choice that I make,

I shape my destiny,

And though the journey may be hard,

I have the power to set myself free.

I will choose to live with purpose

And follow my heart's desires,

For in the end, it's not the destination

But the journey that truly inspires.

"A man who believes in freedom will do anything under the sun to acquire, or preserve his freedom."

\-   Malcolm X

The Courage to Follow Your Heart

The road to our dreams can be winding,

With obstacles that seem insurmountable,

But when we have the courage to follow our heart,

We can overcome anything that is formidable.

The doubts and fears that once held us back,

Will lose their grip as we take the leap,

And though we may stumble and fall,

We'll rise again, stronger and more complete.

So, let your heart be your compass,

As you navigate life's twists and turns,

And trust that every step you take,

Will bring you closer to the life you yearn.

With courage as your constant companion,

And faith in your inner strength,

You'll find that nothing can stop you,

As you follow your heart's intent.

"Dare to believe that good things are possible when you follow your heart."

- Bryant McGill

From Poverty to Prosperity

From poverty to prosperity,

My journey was a long and winding road,

But with each step, I found clarity,

And the courage to break free from the mould.

I grew up with nothing but struggle,

In a world that seemed to be against me,

But I refused to let my dreams crumble,

And let my spirit soar wild and free.

Education became my saving grace,

My key to unlocking a brighter tomorrow,

I studied hard with a fierce pace,

And let my passion fuel my ambition's glow.

I never lost sight of my destination,

And worked tirelessly to make my way,

With each step, I found inspiration,

And let my tenacity pave the way.

The path was rocky and the climb was steep,

But I persisted with all my might,

And every time I faced a defeat,

I rose again, like a phoenix taking flight.

And now I stand tall and proud,

A symbol of hope and resilience,

For I know that with hard work allowed,

Any dream can become a reality's brilliance.

From poverty to prosperity,

I made the journey with unwavering faith,

And now I live life with full clarity,

As my dreams become my life's beautiful wraith.

"Poverty was the greatest motivating factor in my life."

-    Jimmy Dean

Final Words

We have come to the end of the book, and I hope that I have been able to inspire you. Throughout, I hope that the poems and the quotes that I have shared will help you on your own journey.

I have used, and continue to use, many of these poems as part of my daily mantra—a reminder to keep my eye on the ball and to keep chasing my dreams. You can do the same. Read this book as many times and as often you like or need to.

No matter what your current circumstances are, it is not impossible to break free and become everything that you have ever dreamed of. I am still working on my dream, working hard to achieve everything my mind has conceived and confirmed to be good for me; and I keep dreaming, coming up with new goals and new things I want to experience.

For now, I want to leave you with my own quote:

I was born poor but I refuse to spend the rest of my life in poverty, so I will hone my gifts and become everything that I have ever imagined possible.

I want the same for you and wish you the very best. I hope that you will take the time to read my next book.

Until next time...

Marlon McIntyre

About the Author

Marlon McIntyre is a Jamaican-born accountant, poet, and motivational speaker. He was born and raised in one of Jamaica's most notorious ghettoes, where he experienced the challenges of poverty and gang violence. Despite these odds, Marlon believed in the power of education and worked tirelessly to earn his high school diploma and later, his accounting degree through online studies.

Now a successful accountant, Marlon is passionate about inspiring young adults to rise above their struggles and pursue their dreams. Through his poetry and motivational speeches, he shares his personal story of resilience and perseverance, and encourages others to believe in themselves and their potential to create a better future.

Marlon hopes that his first book, *From Poverty to Prosperity: Poems of Hope and Resilience,* will touch the hearts of readers around the world and inspire many to overcome their own obstacles. In his free time, Marlon enjoys reading, writing, and spending time with his family.